Copyright © 2020 by Ingo Blum
www.ingoblumbooks.com

published by planetOh concepts GmbH, Cologne, Germany
www.planetohconcepts.com - info@planet-oh.com

Publisher`s Note:
Please note that the Spanish and English versions of the story were written to be as close as possible. However, in some cases they may differ in order to accomodate the nuances and fluidity of each language. Author, translator, and publisher made every effort to ensure accuracy.

Illustrated by Ira Baykovska
Book layout by Emy Farella
Translation by Carmen Breval
Proofread by Natalia Sepúlveda Adorno

First Edition 2022 - ISBN 979-8840436967

Join my newsletter and get 5 ebooks for FREE at
bit.ly/5freebooks

Ingo Blum

¡Salva el Mundo!

Es el único planeta, que tiene Chocolate.

Save the World!

It is the only planet that has Chocolate.

Illustrated by
Ira Baykovska

Bilingual
English
Spanish

Once there was a little boy.
He was a victim of a war.
He had to run away with his
parents from the place he
was born.

Hubo una vez un niño.
Fue víctima de una guerra.
Tuvo que escapar con sus padres
del lugar donde nació.

He met a soldier who said to him, "Save the world! It's the only planet that has chocolate!" And he gave the boy some chocolate.

En el camino, se encontró con un soldado que le dijo:

—¡Salva el mundo! ¡Es el único planeta que tiene chocolate!—.

Y le dio al niño un poco de chocolate.

He came to a **big city** that he did not know.

Llegó a una **gran ciudad** que no conocía.

He went to a school
where the other kids did
not like him.
The boy was lonely.

Fue a un **colegio** donde no agradaba
a **los otros niños**.
El niño se sentía **solo**.

His teacher said,

"Kindness can change the world."
Save the world because
Kindness is special.

—La bondad puede cambiar el mundo
—dijo su **maestro**.
Salva al mundo porque **la bondad es especial**.

The boy was tired of being alone. But, as he looked around for a friend, he saw he was not the only boy who seemed to feel lonely.

El niño estaba cansado de sentirse solo. Pero, cuando se puso a buscar un amigo cerca, se dio cuenta de que no era el único niño que parecía sentirse solo.

He shared his chocolate with the other lonely boy, and they became friends.
Save the world because friends are important.

Compartió chocolate con otro niño que también se sentía solo y se hicieron amigos.
Salva el mundo porque los amigos son importantes.

The boy grew up.

He was a young man now.

He found a job.

El niño creció. Ahora era un **hombre joven**.

Encontró un **trabajo**.

He met a *girl* he loved.

Conoció a una **chica** a la que quería.

He married her.

At their wedding, they had a
big chocolate cake.

Chocolate was still wonderful,
but not as sweet as his wife.

Se casó con ella.

En su **boda**, tuvieron un enorme
pastel de chocolate.

El chocolate seguía siendo
maravilloso, pero no tan dulce
como su esposa.

Eventually, he had children of his own. And he told them about the Sweets of life.

"It is love, **kindness**, **friendship**, and **peace**," he said.

Con el tiempo, tuvo sus propios hijos. Y les habló acerca de los **dulces de la vida**.

—Es el **amor**, la **bondad**, la **amistad** y la **paz** —les dijo.

The joy of his kids gave him happiness. He remembered the soldier's words but added to them.
Save the world, your children deserve it!

La **alegría** de sus hijos le hizo feliz.

Recordó las palabras del soldado, pero les añadió algo más.

Salva al mundo, los niños se lo merecen.

The years passed.
The boy, who was once a
young man, grew older.
And so did his family.

Los años pasaron.

El niño, que alguna vez fue un
hombre joven, se hizo **mayor**.

También su familia.

He saw his kids grow.

His parents die.

And the country change.

Vio a sus hijos **crecer**.

A sus padres morir.

Y al **país** cambiar.

Then, another war came
and changed everything.
The boy, who was now an
old man, stood at his door
and saw some soldiers
passing by.

Después, otra guerra llegó y lo
cambió todo.
El niño, que ahora era un anciano,
se paró ante su puerta y vio pasar
a algunos soldados.

The old man approached one soldier and said, "Save the world! It is the only place that has chocolate. Return back home, because **peace** shall be for everyone." And he gave the soldier some chocolate.

Se acercó a un soldado y le dijo:

—¡Salva el mundo! Es el único planeta que tiene chocolate. ¡Vuelve a casa, porque la **paz** será para todos!

Y le dio al soldado un poco de chocolate—.

PICS

TO

COLOR

Bilingual Books to Remember

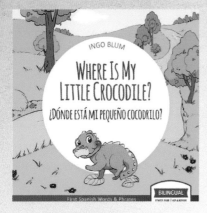

ISBN 978-1983139369

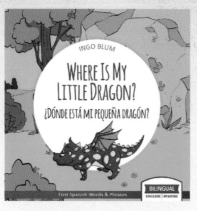

ISBN 978-1983139826

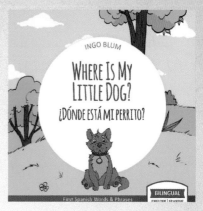

ISBN 978-1983140907

ISBN 979-8695318401

Follow me

Get my 5 eBook Starter
Library in English for FREE on
bit.ly/5freebooks